Where Did You Go To My Pretty Maid?

and other stories of mystery, romance and intrigue

written by
Richard Ford

Where Did You Go To My Pretty Maid?
and other stories of mystery, romance and intrigue

Copyright © Richard Ford 2012

ISBN 978-0-9569208-2-9

First Published December 2012
Published by Design Marque

Printed in Great Britain by
www.designmarque.co.uk

FOREWORD

(By Rhoda Skuce)

The Author of these varied short stories, Richard Ford was inspired to write them from the experiences of many events which have occurred in his own life, many of which he has related to me personally.

For the last 12 years or so, Richard has lived in Pembrokeshire in West Wales and this book is his latest publication since his move here in mid 2000. Prior to this book of short stories, Richard wrote a book about a Fox and his friends entitled 'Matty the Fox'-An imaginative book of stories about little 'Human Animals'. He has also published a book of his poems as well as a faith inspired, apologetic book on Christianity.

However, this book of 8 short stories is quite a departure from all Richard's other works, as these are stories of Mystery, Intrigue and Romance. Just the sort of reading for people of a certain age who like to delve into a short story at bedtime.

I have known Richard for about 9 years and during this time I have always considered him to be a constant and helpful friend and one I have not only encouraged, but have shown interest in, both in himself and in his work as a Writer.

This is a book full of stories, I have already read and thoroughly enjoyed, as I am sure you will too.

Rhoda Skuce

DEDICATION

To all those people amongst my friends, family and school colleagues who were an influence and an inspiration in the writing of these stories.

ACKNOWLEDGEMENTS

Rhoda Skuce, Jennifer Mahoney, Alec Vowles, Vicky Vowles, Alan Hunter, Ray Harford, June Ashdown, Christopher Power, Sarah Ray.
Also to various family members and old school colleagues who are covertly hidden among the pages, although possibly unrecognisable to them.

Contents

Where Did You Go To My Pretty Maid?

Where Did You Go To My Pretty Maid?

The scream must have been heard by everyone in the vicinity of the cottage. Aunt Freda almost tripped over the body as she made her way down the garden path that autumn evening. She glanced at the slight figure of a seemingly young red-haired girl, throat cut from ear to ear, blood pouring down her blouse. Freda's eyes popped out, her mouth sagged open. She attempted a scream but at first nothing emanated from her lips. She turned, staggering wildly towards the cottage, hands groping in front of her. Running into the kitchen, she banged the door behind her. It was only then that the ear piercing scream exploded from her mouth, but Freda herself failed to hear it as immediately afterwards she lost consciousness and fell into a heap onto the stone floor.

Aunt Freda had always been a complex character. She was fastidious and a perfectionist to the extreme. Everything about her looked correct, her clothes, her make-up, her hair. She was infinitely well groomed and appeared exactly right for any and every occasion. Her home and garden were also immaculate, nothing ever out of place and a place for everything. Unfortunately she expected similar standards from everyone she came in contact with. If there were things in her world that she didn't like, but were outside of her control to change, she just pretended they didn't exist. In a sense she looked at the world through eyes that saw things as she wanted to see them and was completely oblivious to her own spitefulness and often sadistic behaviour.

Being both prudish, puritanical and apparently devoid of any humour, she was also harsh and relentless in her pursuance of what she imagined in her own mind, was perfection. Seemingly possessed with a sort of ungodly, uncharitable power, she certainly never accepted fools gracefully and she made a truly formidable school-teacher, no patience, no compassion whatsoever. I, myself had been taught by her as a boy and the fact that I was her nephew did me no favours. She taught me during the war years when even toilet paper was rationed. It was issued to you from a cupboard on request and if you dared voice a complaint that two sheets of rough bronco styled paper were insufficient for your needs, you were met with a cold icy stare and the likelihood of a sharp cuff around the ear. As it was, Aunt Freda seemed to take a personal delight if, in her opinion, the wrong answer was given by any unsuspecting school chum, she would pounce on them like a vulture, grab her wooden ruler, roll up their sleeves and give two hearty thwacks across the wrists of her victims. Even I had experienced the suffering of such brutality and God did it hurt?

No one, not even my mother, appeared to like Freda. She had never married, breaking off the one and only relationship that anyone knew about, when she began to suspect that her would be husband might not always be willing to succumb to her controlling nature. She seemed not to mind being disliked, in fact perversely, appeared to enjoy it. She was so self righteous, we always believed Aunt Freda considered herself somewhere above the rest of the human race!

Poor Freda, I suppose she had to be pitied! Freda eventually came to. Not a sound could be heard. She groped hazily for the light switch in the now darkened room, at the same time running a finger over quite a large bump on the back of her head. Her arms ached severely. She noticed two nasty bruises already appearing on her elbows. Freda felt sick, cold and extremely nervous.

The memory of the enormity of what she'd seen came flooding back to her. She walked carefully into the front room and picked up a poker from the hearth. Quite what for she didn't really know. She then grabbed a coat and torch from the hallway and made her way slowly out into the garden. The torch had a strong beam and she flashed it all over the path and the garden itself. To her utter amazement, the body had disappeared. No trace, except some blood stains where she had noticed the body originally. It was starting to rain, soon all signs, even of that, would be gone.

'Oh what to do ? No one would ever believe me. Those fools of policemen down at the station can't even find a lost cat. They don't like me anyway, I know they don't. They'll think I'm mad. I'm not. I'm not' Suddenly without warning Freda did something she never did. She started sobbing. The tears, a few at first, became prolific as she sat down on the garden seat and cried as if there were no tomorrow.

How long she sat there, she wasn't sure. All she knew was that she felt really ill. Her head throbbed. There were pains behind the eyes and yes, for the first time that she could remember, she felt afraid, really afraid.

Freda made her way back into the house and despite her heavy coat, fell shivering onto the settee. She awoke to sunlight streaming into her room, the dark coloured curtains still open from the night before.

Gently lifting her legs off from the settee, Freda peered at herself in the mirror 'What a sight' she murmured to herself. She did, however, feel a little better. Moving into the kitchen, she filled the kettle. After a hot mug of tea, she felt some colour returning to her cheeks. She tried to pull herself together 'A plan of action' she said to herself. Glancing at the clock she noticed it was 7.30 'Got to be in school in an hour' Freda sat at the table, head in hands 'My confidence has gone, I must go in, no I can't go in'. Tears came to her eyes again 'Who was that girl? Certainly no one I could recognise from school and how could her body be there one hour and not the next? I can't get it together' she thought. 'Perhaps I'm going mad, having hallucinations but no, the blood, the blood was still there on the ground, even if the body wasn't'

Freda went out into the garden again. It

had been raining but even so one could still make out small flecks of blood on the footpath.

She glanced at her watch, 8a.m. She suddenly decided to run down to the nearby phone box. Picking up the phone, she put some coins in the slot and dialled a number 'Mrs Evenden? It's Freda, Freda Halsworthy. I'm so sorry Mrs Evenden, I can't come in today I'm afraid. I, I've had a fall, slipped on a rug and badly banged my head. No I'll be ok. No need for the doctor I'll just take it easy for a couple of days. I should be in by Thursday, mild concussion I should imagine'

Freda replaced the receiver and walked slowly home. She felt lonely, uncertain. 'Why all these new emotions? She'd never felt lonely or lacking in confidence before. When was the last time she'd cried'? She couldn't remember.

'I'm scared' she thought, 'so afraid and still weepy', 'shock' she tried to tell herself 'I've had a severe shock - be alright tomorrow' She arrived at her door. 'Another cup of tea, that'll do it' She let herself into her cottage and moved into the kitchen. Pulling her shoulders back, she tried to summon up some courage but try as she may, Freda realised she couldn't cope. 'Must talk to someone' she thought, 'But who and exactly what do I say to them'?

Freda sipped her tea 'I know, Mary Sallinger down the road. She's always polite and smiling. Someone I always feel I could trust. Yes I'm sure she'll be ok I'll call and see Mary'.

A few minutes later found Freda knocking on Mary's door. Mary Sallinger was an elderly lady, a retired widow. At one time she and her husband had owned and run a local florists' so Mary was used to meeting and dealing with all sorts of people.

'Why Miss Halsworthy, What a surprise, do come in' said Mary ushering Freda over the doorstep. She paused, noticing Freda's grim and pale look 'Is there something the matter'? 'I've had a shock' muttered Freda, 'A nasty, cruel shock and it's left me' she broke off suddenly overcome by another flood of tears.

'Dear oh dear' said Mary, 'Come now dry your eyes and tell me all about it while I make us a pot of tea' She took a handkerchief from her sleeve and offered it to Freda. Freda was thinking about the young dead girl and the profound effect it was having on her. She was remembering herself at about the same age 'I dare not risk confiding in Mary. It must never come out' she decided. 'No way could she cope with being the centre of a police enquiry. She had her reputation to consider' Freda imagined the line of questioning from the police 'You say you have never suffered from delusions'? And then with scepticism, 'You are a teetotaller you say'?

Freda shuddered visibly. She was Freda Halsworthy, she might not be particularly liked but at least she commanded some form of respect in the village.

'More tea dear'? Her thoughts broke off as she noticed Mary about to pour another cup. 'What you need is some fellowship, all alone in that cottage. Now I won't take no for an answer. You must come along with me to one of our little evenings the ladies in the village hold. It's Mrs Turner's turn this week. We are having a talk on French Cookery'. Freda shuddered again but nevertheless decided perhaps she would go. After all she needed to keep her mind off what happened. 'Alright I'll be there' she found herself saying.

Gradually in the ensuing weeks and months Freda's life changed dramatically. She even gave ladies' evenings herself and sometimes, she herself became the speaker for the occasion. Freda was very learned and able and found herself thoroughly enjoying talking to the ladies' of the village on a wide variety of subjects.

Her confidence returned but with it came a new kind of humility as she not only relied on others for her new found joy but received and returned friendship instead of animosity. She became much less lonely, less self reliable, but also happier as she adapted and adjusted to the new person who had been lurking inside of her.

Despite discreet enquiries on her behalf and a continual scan of the newspapers for any news of missing persons, foul play or whatever, the mystery of the body remained unsolved.

Over the years, the memory of it all happening dwindled and faded and ceased to become a problem for her. By now Freda had settled into a peaceful retirement, tending her garden, visiting what had become new friends, and involving herself amicably into the community life of the village. She was content.

Twenty or so years after the mysterious body had been dumped in Freda's garden, the owner of a small café, several miles away overheard the conversation between two men, probably in their early thirties, chatting at a table whilst sipping coffee.

'How did you do it'? one of them was asking

'My elder brother works for a company of waxwork manufacturers who regularly get tenders from Madame Tussauds' in London. He was at my school too and experienced at first hand how vicious his aunt could be, cruel, vindictive, ruler slapping. He'd really suffered under her as we all had. We knew where she lived, that she was on her own and how she enjoyed wandering around her garden at sunset. Her garden looks out onto open ground. There was a high wall between the two. It was simple really, a hired van, a waxwork, a wig, masses of lovely pig's blood, you know the sort you can buy from theatrical shops. We devised the whole plan to scare her as she had scared us. The idea of removing the body later was a stroke of pure genius. I've no sympathy for her at all, wicked old witch. I wonder if it worked'? He laughed. 'I suppose we'll never know will we'?

The Song

The Song

It was a warm afternoon that summer
by the river that flowed gently into the sea
beyond. The estuary which curled inland on
their right, was ablaze with multi-coloured
sails and flags which were flapping noisily
against their masts, seemingly in tune with
each other, an orchestra of yachts playing a
gentle tapping rhythm. The sky was blue, a
few wisps of cloud floating gently in a light
breeze. Flocks of gulls were diving for fish that
only they could see, their calls expressing their
delight at the kill of their prey. To Debbie and
Andrew this particular spot was heaven. A long
discovered trysting place where their romance
had been given a chance to develop and grow
in spite of Andrew's father's fear that his son
was too young to get so emotionally involved
with one of his employees' daughters. At
least this was the official reason for Andrew's
indifferent, almost rude attitude to Debbie.
However Andrew knew that there was a deeper
motive, one of prejudice that his son, who one
day would inherit his business, was 'dallying
around' as he put it with a labourers daughter.

Andrew had long ago come to terms with
his father's snobbish attitude and had pushed

it into the back of his mind. This afternoon was no exception. He bluntly refused to let his father's pomposity ruin an idyllic romance. Andrew loved Debbie with a burning intensity that was a surprise even to him. Nothing was more important to him than the trembling emotion that rose up inside him every time he looked at her. Whenever he nervously unbuttoned her blouse, he felt his fingers were experiencing some sort of mild tingling electric shock. A bead of perspiration would break out on his forehead at her touch and a tiny droplet of spittle would moisten the corner of his lips.

So far they had managed to control themselves. 'No Andrew' Debbie had often said. 'No, Not yet' but the magic spell that was being weaved around them this particular afternoon appeared to have a power all of its own forcing past boundaries to be broken, emotions overtaken by sheer desire, passion but also real love. Nothing could block these feelings. Feelings that were so strong that mere survival necessitated there being fully expressed.

Two screeching gulls swooped down over their heads in affirmation and appraisal as flesh melted into flesh, their bodies locking together in consummation of this their first love.

Several minutes later, passions spent Andrew leaned back sighing contentedly whilst Debbie combed her long black hair with her fingertips. Andrew glanced tenderly with concern towards Debbie. 'Are you O.K'? he asked. She smiled back blushing slightly. 'Oh yes' she said. Her eyes looking into his with admiration.

'Iv'e written a song for you' said Andrew 'Oh it's not very good and it's unfinished really but it expresses just a fragment of what I feel for you. Do you want to hear it'? Debbie nodded her approval as Andrew took out a small sheet of paper from his inside pocket. 'O.K' he laughed. 'Here goes then

"Oh baby what you doin' to me?
I love you, It's as plain as can be,
Please will you, Oh why don't you love me?
Oh my pretty baby doll.
I saw you just the other night
Sat by the window, bathed in the light
Golly honey what a beautiful sight.
Oh my pretty baby doll
My pretty baby doll."

'What's all this baby doll bit?' said Debbie 'Have you been watching that Carroll Baker film? Give it here. I do like it and it will be a wonderful keep sake' She tucked it into her handbag. 'That's an unusual bag' said Andrew. 'It's more so than you think' said Debbie holding. up a green mottled leather bag. 'It's got a pocket within a pocket, see? I'll put this' indicating the song 'in here'.

They stayed watching the sunset over the river. The wind had dropped and the tap tap of sail on mast had been reduced to an occasional flutter. The rhythm now gone. They walked slowly back to the village. Both feeling content and absolute in each other's company. 'I want this moment to last for ever' said Andrew 'Oh yes' said Debbie. 'How does one stop time moving forward'? She gripped his arm tightly, fearful of letting go. Some weeks later Andrew received his call up papers. He was to report at Cardington in Bedfordshire at 1.45 p.m on 14th October 'Only eight more weeks' said Andrew to himself. His relationship with his father had improved recently. 'It was as though' thought Andrew 'Dad is assuming my relationship with Debbie will peter out whilst I am doing my two years National Service in the R.A.F., then when I return, I'll be groomed into Dad's business and Debbie, he hopes, will be past history'. During the two months that followed, Andrew and Debbie took every possible opportunity to spend time at their special place. Their love grew and matured although the joy of that first encounter when he had presented Debbie with 'The Song' was never reached again. Instead an even more meaningful and deeper relationship had grown between them.

The day finally came. Debbie came to see Andrew off on the train. Dad didn't come. He had said his goodbye's early that morning before setting off to his business. Tears flowed down Debbie's cheeks 'You will write, often, won't you'? she said. Andrew nodded, a lump in his throat, his emotions fluctuating madly between the deep sadness he felt about losing her, coupled with an excitement about the possibilities this new adventure might hold. Soon Debbie was just a blur on the horizon far down the platform as the train steamed rapidly along the track. The repetition of the noise of train on rails seeming to signify an uncertainty of the next chapter in their lives.

At first the letters flowed frequently between them but a dispute between Debbie and Andrew's father's resulted in both a job change and Debbie moving several hundred miles away. Andrew also, after eight weeks of 'square bashing', was moved first to the Blackpool area for Catering training then again and yet again in fairly rapid postings. Eventually the inevitable happened without either if them realising why or how, Andrew and Debbie lost touch. Andrew was discharged sixteen months later and settled down at home in his fathers' business as the firm's Catering Manager.

Eventually he married Helen, a girl he met on a trip to London and they bought a house three or four streets away from Dad.

They appeared happy enough at first but he never forgot Debbie. He realised that there was a void in his life, an ache when he allowed himself to remember their time together but he never tried to trace her, feeling that what he might find would altogether be too painful. No, better let things be.
Andrew and Helen's marriage finally faltered after their only child Carol was killed in a car crash when only seventeen years old. Carol had gone to a Tennis Club ball, at a small town ten miles north of their home. The boy driving them back afterwards, had apparently overtaken a car which itself had swerved to avoid a cat. Kevin, the driver, had been drinking and as he hit a curb, their car did a complete somersault. Unfortunately, Carol sitting in the passenger seat was the only one

who was killed.

Helen never recovered from the shock. She had doted on Carol and projected all her feelings of guilt and remorse onto Andrew, unreasonably blaming him for allowing Carol to go to the party.

From then on their marriage dwindled away rapidly until there was only animosity left between them. Andrew's father had died sometime previously and Andrew had taken over the business.

After the divorce Andrew decided to sell up and move to a small town, Althorne in Essex, where he took over the Catering in the only hotel of any size in the area.

He never married again but became very involved in the community projects of the town, also indulging himself in his long neglected passion for writing. Occasionally he also dabbled in oils, tended his garden, was elected onto various committees, frequented his local, sometimes attended the Parish Church and settled down to a fairly routine existence, but he never forgot Debbie. One day on impulse, he decided to return to the special place where they had made love that first time. He sat on the bench remembering his time there with Debbie more than fifty years ago and the day of unimaginable ecstasy they had enjoyed together.

'Why hadn't he tried to trace her or her him? Fear of disappointment? Had she forgotten him? Probably a grandmother several times over now' he thought. 'If she were alive at all'

'Was he crazy? Why should a now sixty-eight year old woman still be interested in what was then a gawky teenager? How did two people who were so earnest about each other lose touch'? Questions pervaded his mind. His emotions haunted him.

'I wouldn't know her now' he thought 'even if she were still alive. I'm quite insane. Why should I want to get in touch anyway? My own marriage was a disaster, ending up losing both wife and daughter'.

He drove dejectedly back to Althorne and tried to turn his mind back to the events of the week.

Andrew was supposed to be organising the local Rotary Club car boot and jumble sale for the following Saturday. 'I had better start preparing the inner hall tables so that everyone knows what we aim to sell from which table' he muttered to himself.

Some days later, Margaret Southon, the Rotary Club secretary was busy in the hall unpacking boxes.

'Andrew' she said. 'Do you want all leather goods together or the handbags with handbags and belts with belts and other haberdashery'?

'Oh you must choose' said Andrew who was pre-occupied with determining quite what the object he was holding in his hand was used for. He looked up. Suddenly it was as if a thick black curtain was being parted to show the transparent nets behind. 'Where did you find that handbag'? he said pointing to the one Margaret was holding. 'It came with boxes of stuff. I have no idea where from' said Margaret.

Andrew grasped the handbag. His fingers were trembling. 'This was madness. Despite its unusual design and colour, there were doubtless many others similar to it. It couldn't be a one off could it? Was it the one'? Memories of himself as a young man making love on a beautiful beach flooded his mind. 'A pocket within a pocket' Debbie had said. Hands shaking he pressed the catch. Fifty years old, the handbag, though worn, still had style, character. He reached inside and unzipped one pocket, then another. Andrew felt Debbie's presence everywhere. This was nothing short of miraculous. He opened the neatly folded sheet of notepaper.

"Oh Baby what you doin to me" Even the words were apt. 'What are you doing to me'? Andrew mumbled to himself. 'I must find you Debbie' he said 'I will. Even if you are gone. I must know, wherever, whenever. We are meant to meet again. Oh what a fool I've been. The wasted years. Why? What did I fear? Why was I so worried about finding you? Whatever did I expect'? Tears were rolling down his cheeks.

'I'm sorry Margaret' he said. 'I must take this. I need to trace the donor. Please forgive me' He rushed out of the hall and down the steps, not even considering where he might be going.

Just as he was running down the driveway, another helper, Anne, saw Andrew grasping the handbag. 'Where are you off to with that' she said. 'I'm trying to find out who donated it' he said. 'I can tell you that' said Anne, 'Mrs Smethurst. I remember her bringing it in. It's so unusual'

'Thanks' said Andrew. He jumped into his car and hastily drove to the Smethursts' house.

'Oh yes' said Mrs Smethurst greeting him at the door. 'But it wasn't mine originally.

I bought it at another sale in Maldon, at a school, Breckington School. I realised after I had bought it that it wouldn't really go with anything I've got as an accessory. In any case it was beginning to look a bit worn so I gave it to the Rotary Club'.

'Oh Heavens' said Andrew. 'Well at least the school will still be open. I'll go and see the Head now. Perhaps he'll know where it came from. How long ago did you buy it'?

'Only very recently' said Mrs Smethurst. 'I hope you find whatever it is you are looking for' she added as he rushed off.

The Headmaster of Breckington School was out but the Assistant Head thought that the handbag had come in a pile of Bric-a-Brac from Lady Merton at Gangs' Valley House. He gave Andrew directions and soon a portly gentleman was answering the front door of a rather forbidding Victorian Mansion.

'I'll get the housekeeper' he said as Andrew gave a brief explanation of his quest.

Suddenly Andrew felt as if he had just stepped out of a time machine. There was no mistaking it. It was Debbie. Plumper, grey hair, but still beautiful and totally recognisable and not wearing a wedding ring, Debbie.

She looked up as she came to the door,

a flicker of recognition appearing across her face. She looked first at Andrew, then at the handbag, recognition mixing with bewilderment.

'Andrew, my bag. Where on earth did you get it? Andrew it can't be you. It is you. Oh I don't understand' Tears came into her eyes. She trembled slightly. She stuttered nervously, unsure of what to say. 'That's my bag. I found it at the back of a cupboard when I was sorting out things for the jumble sale. It must have got mixed in with the items they picked up and by the time I realised it, it had been sold and I had no idea who the purchaser was. It was empty except for the song you wrote for me. I never did want to clutter it up with anything other than that as the song was so special to me. I really thought that I had lost it. Where did you find it? How did you? Oh I don't understand' She broke off.

'Debbie' said Andrew softly. 'Get your hat and coat. I've come to take you for a drive. Perhaps you can guess where? First though. Let's eat. Where is the best restaurant in Maldon? I hope you can get off duty for a few hours. We've got fifty years to catch up on. Come on'.

Fat Mick

Fat Mick

The rain was falling heavily as I stood
at the graveside and watched as four burly
men lowered Fat Mick's coffin into a newly dug
grave. My lips were quivering and although
I was crying inside in a sort of parallel to
the raindrops around me, no actual tears
could come. Instead, an almost unbearable
heaviness and deep sadness gripped my soul.
Sat by me, Fat Mick's black and white collie
'Badger' whined pitifully, seemingly in both
time and tune to the sound of ropes pulling
around the dark wooden coffin. Finally, as it
hit the earth with a bump, Badger's whining
ceased. The dog looked up at me questioningly
as I drew the lead nearer to my side. 'He
knew, of course he knew' I thought, 'but he
didn't understand. How could he?
'Join the club' I whispered to Badger for I had
no more understanding than he.
My mind went back to the day three
years prior. I had been walking slowly down
Berwick Street market in London early one
June day. Having always been interested in
antiques, I had been told of a wonderful stall

where they apparently sold old brass and copper candlesticks.

It was a warm, cloudless day and the atmosphere in this bustling market was noisy but friendly.

My attention was drawn to a very large man sitting against the wall on a pavement between two stalls in the centre of the market. He was selling copies of 'The Big Issue' and seemed rather anxious, his huge frame not only partially blocking the walkway, but also casting an eerie shadow across the road itself. I took in his appearance, sallow skin, bearded and moustached and showing a glimpse of slightly protruding white teeth. His hair looked slightly unkempt and I noticed his deeply cracked fingers. His clothes appeared misshapen and ill fitting, but his eyes betrayed a humour beyond their apparent sadness. I felt drawn to this man. But it was the dog that struck me even more. A black and white Collie who was sidled up close to his master striking a protective pose, despite his obvious nervousness. The dog appeared to be saying 'This is my Dad. I am looking after him so don't try anything or you will have me to answer to'.

I purchased a copy of 'The Big Issue',

risked patting Badger as I learned he was called and I was about to turn away when some totally inexplicable impulse caused me to say to the fat man 'Care for a drink'? As soon as I had said it I wondered why but by then it was to late to retract. 'It's ok' I added answering the man's unasked question. 'I know a pub just around the back of here where dogs are welcome' The man waved a bundle of ' Big issues' vaguely in front of me as if to say 'I've got to sell these' ' You've got to eat' I said 'Both of you' looking at Badger. 'It's ok. Come on'.

We made our way to the 'Bunch of Grapes' in Costa street and started to chat. Arriving at the pub, I ordered a pint of creamflow each plus three turkey sandwiches, one of course for 'Badger'.

That morning was the start of a warm and deep friendship between three people. Of course I am referring to Badger as a person. All my life I have felt a sense of instinctive awareness and compassion both for animals and people. I knew Fat Mick had a story to tell, a story, which I was sure would include some painful episodes and ones which I felt would mirror my own pain, now thankfully in the past.

In the days and weeks that followed,

fragments and portions of 'Fat Mick's' story were revealed. He had been brought up as an only child, on a farm in Suffolk. As a young lad he'd loved it there amongst the animals. Always a dog, cats but mostly cattle, together with a few sheep and pigs and a gaggle of truly ferocious geese. Geese, which he had delighted in gently teasing by pulling faces at them and hollering, then suddenly and unexpectedly turning on his heels to see if they could catch him when they chased after him.

Although he had very few friends he never felt lonely as like 'Dr. Doolittle' he enjoyed talking to the animals. Apart from which there were always farm hands working there day by day with whom he could chat. It was an idyllic existence. No worries or cares, a veritable paradise. He loved the farm and the only shadows were when the pigs were killed or cows were sold. He knew each one and they all had individual names and their own personalities Harvest time also, was very enjoyable, potato picking, blackberry and apple picking and helping his mother wrap the newly picked Cox's orange pippins in newspaper, laying them in neat rows, not touching, in a dry flat attic space to ripen. Fat Mick's stories and anecdotes of rural life on the farm were interesting, multifarious, and often funny, too many I'm afraid to recount here.

One afternoon he had an hilarious adventure, attempting to milk dear 'Bessie', the cow by hand. She'd obviously resented this bitterly as she had moo'd in a very complaining fashion and squirted her milk all over his face and eyes, as well as his clothes, to the annoyance of his mother. He never attempted it again. Another day he learned that geese could give rather nasty bites. I say bite rather than peck for that is what it was. Fortunately for Fat Mick, the pressure brought to bear by Millie the goose was rather less than it might have been as she had attempted to enforce it whilst running across their front lawn and was fortunately unable to get a firm grip on his hand.

I laughed hearing these and other stories so was not really prepared for the horror to come. Suddenly like the 'Black Hole' ride at one of those theme parks, I was thrust unto a tragically dark area of 'Fat Mick's' life.

Apparently it was a rather foggy January morning. Fat Mick's father had gone to market very early with a few cattle. The remainder of farm hands either hadn't yet arrived or were scattered about working in other parts of the farm. Only Fat Mick's parents, Badger and some cats were in the big farmhouse at the top of the lane.

Suddenly, without warning, the door was flung open and two thick set men with scarves around their mouths and noses burst into the room.

Perhaps they didn't think anyone would be up, although the light was on. Anyway one of them brandished a gun at Fat Mick's mother and in a hoarse voice reminiscent of an 'Edward G Robinson' gangster movie, the type often seen on T.V, cried out 'Where do you keep the cash'? Even as he spoke the intruder noticed the small wall safe on one side of the room 'Tie her up Smiley' he said 'And him too'. We don't want any interference from these two. Badger was barking furiously but was doing little else to help.

Both Fat Mick's father and his mother had then been gagged and trussed up like Christmas turkeys and then the safe had been shot at in an attempt to open it. But much worse was about to follow. As the shots were being fired, Fat Mick had arrived home unexpectedly. Apparently the opening of the market had been postponed owing to thick fog.

In a flash and in what was certainly a

reflex action, the man shooting at the safe turned suddenly and fired at Fat Mick's father. The bullet hit the side of his temple and he slumped heavily to the ground. A muffled scream came from behind Fat Mick's mother's gag.

Both intruders quickly fled in a panic. Fat Mick and his mother could do nothing but look on in horror as his father lay there dead. Six months later, Fat Mick's mother also died from a massive stroke brought on, it was assumed, by the severe trauma and anxiety she had suffered on that fateful day.

Fat Mick's life was never to be the same again. Of course he inherited the farm, the farm which he had once loved but which had now become a prison and a tomb to him.

The publicity surrounding the story of what had happened there made it difficult to sell.

Fat Mick coped for a while as best as he could, but in time the stress of all that had happened and of managing the farm single handed, caused him to become so severely depressed and unable to cope that the day came when he realised that he would either have to sell or destroy all his beloved animals, except Badger whom he had had for just two years and to walk out for good. With just a suitcase and not a great deal of money, as there were many outstanding debts, he came to London.

In his depressed state of mind he opted for a job where he felt he would be under less pressure, selling copies of 'The Big Issue'.

It would seem that things improved somewhat on his meeting 'Millie', a rather pretty girl from one of the fruit and vegetable stalls in the market, Unfortunately she had a demanding voracious sexual appetite. They had a brief affair but as Fat Mick bluntly confessed, 'her expectations really did exceed my capacity' I think what Fat Mick decided he really needed was to have a good friend.

After Millie there were times when he had felt quite suicidal but he was never driven to contemplate it seriously. He remembered, he told me once, the story of the little girl who said when a leaf had fallen off a tree and hit her head, 'Oh the sky has fallen in' 'It's only a leaf dear' her mother had said.' Look the sky is still there'.

'Yes the sky is still there' Fat Mick had said to himself. This obvious fact together with the companionship of Badger, whom he loved, had kept him going through wind and fire.

One day when he was feeling negative and melancholy, a little sparrow flew through the window of his flat and landed on his head. It appeared to be unhurt so he picked it up and let it fly away. It soared upwards flapping its little wings and landed high up on a branch of a tree. Fat Mick pondered on the piece in 'The Bible' which informs us that God cares even for sparrows, although he is concerned even more for His children. This thought led him into considering a well known chorus he remembered learning as a choirboy in the tiny Suffolk Church he had attended with his parents. 'Amazing Grace'. He'd always loved the third verse, especially now as it seemed so relevant and poignant. 'Through many a toil and tear I have already come. It was grace that brought me thus this far and grace will bring me home'

It was to be a prophetic inspiration but not yet. I met Fat Mick three years before he died of natural causes of a sort. I say of a sort as he was decidedly a comfort eater, raiding the fridge with abandonment, particularly when feeling low. The name Fat Mick, had been given to him by his fellow peers in the market after his weight had ballooned from 16 to 19 stone, an increase which had weakened his heart.

The years we had as friends were some of the happiest of my life. Since my wife to be Helen and I had split up just before our proposed wedding many years ago. I believe those years were happy for Fat Mick too. Our friendship of mutual understanding had helped us both to overcome the difficulties of the past.

Apart from spending hours together chatting philosophically over a couple of drinks in our favourite pubs, we often played pool together, joined a local darts team, went on numerous walks and swimming expeditions with Badger. We sometimes went to the cinema or theatre together. On one occasion we even went down to Devon to stay, yes on a farm. It was a partial healing for Fat Mick but the pain was still etched deeply in his face and I watched sadly as the tears rolled down his cheeks one day as he helped feed the pigs.

I tried, I hope with sensitivity, to suggest a return to the farm where he had lived. I felt it might help to lay any ghosts however difficult this might prove to be. 'Not yet Rich, not yet' was all he said. As it happened he was never to return. His death at the end of one of our perfect days, in fact I remember we had been laughing at some ridiculous joke we'd heard somewhere. A heart attack, very quick and then all over.

The noise of the empty hearse engine revving up brought me back with a start. I was alone, save for Badger with my memories. The grave digger levelled off the soil and left. It had stopped raining.

I knelt down by the grave-side. Suddenly the tears came. Welling up in my eyes and spilling helplessly over my previously cracked mouth.

'Goodbye Mick' I said quietly 'God bless you my friend. Be at peace now'

I rose, patted the dog who was slowly wagging his tail. His own personal way of saying. 'Farewell'.

I gently pulled the lead. 'Come on Badger, Come on boy' I said.

Annie The Bag Lady

Annie The Bag Lady

'Get out of 'ere. Go on get out. We don't want the likes of you round 'ere'. The shrill hostile voice echoed in Annie's ear as she shuffled as quickly as she could from the little parade of shops situated at the far end of Arlington Street.

She caught the words 'Bloomin ole 'ag' as she turned the corner and made her way in the direction of Hyde Park Corner. It was very cold that October afternoon and her legs were cramped where she had been sitting for some time begging for money from passers by. Now it had started to rain. Annie caught a reflection of herself in a shop window. What a sight she looked. 'How could one sink so low'? Her battered felt hat seemed to be objecting indignantly at being placed so precariously and ignominiously on top of her head. A few wispy grey hairs stuck out like faded sliced green beans in an ungainly fashion over her ears. Her skin was sallow and pale and looked as if it had never heard of, let alone ever seen any soap. Her nose had a purplish tinge to it like a deep frozen strawberry. Annie's eyes however looked sharp and not devoid of intelligence. The slightly uncontrolled movement in them, giving the impression that they were listening rather than seeing. Annie decided not to bother putting up her umbrella. She had paid all of 7p. for it at a local car boot sale, a mustardy yellow colour with so many holes in it, it looked more like a circle of gruyére cheese than an umbrella. What was more, the rain, Annie decided, always seemed to go through the holes rather than on the few bits of material still clinging on for grim death to the framework.

Annie hoisted her back pack over her shoulders and vainly attempted to pull fingerless gloves over her fingers, fingers that already appeared white with cold. She blew on them raspishly with little or no effect 'Could really do with a cup of tea' she muttered to herself. Suddenly like an answered prayer, a man called out to her from within a nearby stationery refreshment van.

'Wanna cuppa tea love? You look as if you could do with it', seeing Annie's slight hesitation, 'Go orn, no charge. I'm feeling generous' he added. He half smiled. Annie gratefully took the steaming mug of strong tea and drank, the rim, almost burning her

chapped lips. Gulping it down she felt better.
Thanking her benefactor she plodded slowly
on up the street. Several people were mingling
around the pavements. Some of them ignored
her, some looked right through her, one or
two frowned. The odd person showed obvious
disgust, one even spat at her.

'Must sit down' she thought. Annie
paused at the doorway of a shop already shut.
The little entrance porch would provide some
shelter for her from the wind. 'Ere this is my
pitch' a voice cried.

Annie hadn't noticed the strangely
dressed tarty looking woman in the shadows
the other side of the porch 'Shan't get any pick
ups if you sit there' the woman cried, then
more gently looking at Annie. 'Oh go on then.
You can stay for a few minutes. God you look
totally knackered. I've seen dead people with
a better colour than wot you got. Wonna fag
dear? Go on darlin. It ain't dope' Annie puffed
at her cigarette, quickly putting it out as she
began to feel dizzy. 'No offence love' she said to
the prostitute. 'I haven't ad a fag in ages, not
used to 'em. Can't really afford the readies' 'Aw
you poor ole dear. 'Ow much 'ave you made
today then'? Annie counted some coins she'd
stuffed in her anorak pocket '£3 pounds 91'

she said. 'Cor aint much is it'? said Velma introducing herself 'Go on 'ere's a fiver. Don't deal in wonners I don't' Velma suddenly made a move. 'I'm orf, this is a lousy pitch. I'm goin furver up west. Good trade there that's if the cops don't move you on. Ta Ta Ducks. Give yerself a day orf, looks like you could do wiv it' and with a cheery wave she was gone.

Annie settled down as snugly as she could in the doorway of the shop. She wrapped her skirt more closely round her legs. 'What's that smell'? she thought, 'Sweet, sickly'? 'Oh God' she murmured as she hastily removed a sticky lollipop from her leg 'Being in the light isn't much cop' she thought 'Being in the dark isn't either'. It's a no win situation. Oh I noticed a Salvation Army hall up the road. I'll call in and get another cup of tea and maybe a free slice of bread or something. Annie collected her bits together and started up the hill. She felt lonely and damp. Her legs felt numb and stiff. A few tears dribbled down her cheeks. She was beginning to feel really sorry for herself. 'What a bloody awful world it's become' she said. 'No one cares anything, for anybody else, no that's not totally true, some folk are kind, usually the least expected those who have suffered themselves as a rule from others 'unkindnesses' She entered the Salvation Army hall. 'Nobody in here' she thought to herself. 'Oh well'. Suddenly a skinny, prim looking woman with a shiny nose appeared and ushered her in. 'Are you looking for accommodation'? she said to Annie. 'Nah I'm looking for a cuppa tea' said Annie. The skinny woman blinked and led her to a chair by the table. 'I'll bring it over. Would you like a biscuit or -'. Annie nodded and the woman came back with two small biscuits, an unbuttered scone and some rather weak looking tea. 'Nah, rots yer teeth' said Annie smiling and exhibiting a row of blackened teeth.

The skinny woman winced slightly and went away. Annie munched at her over baked scone and poured some tea, first into her saucer and then her mouth. At least it was hot even if it was a bit stewed.

Presently another lady appeared. This one was stout and formal 'Have you met the Lord'? she said in an embarrassed sort of voice 'Lord Who'? said Annie. 'Oh you mean the bloke who runs this place. Is he a lord? I thought the Salvation Army owned it'? 'I mean The Lord' said the fat lady rather impatiently. 'Perhaps you'd like to read this'? She handed

Annie a small tract entitled 'God wants you saved' 'I'll look at it later' Annie said to the embarrassed lady shoving the tract into her pocket. Annie drank her tea, found the thin woman, gave her thanks and ventured out into the early evening. A dog appeared from nowhere yapping and snapping at her ankles. 'Scram, Go away. I like dogs' said Annie 'But not yappy dogs round your ankles'. The dog gave a sudden yelp and ran off whining as Annie's boot inadvertently made direct contact with it's tail. 'Oh Crumbs, now I need a wee' Annie mumbled to herself. 'Why on earth didn't I go in the Salvation Army hall? Well I'm not going back there now that's for sure'
She wandered into Green Street station, picked out a 20p coin from her pocket and went into the personal loo. 'Quite nice' she thought. 'Dry, comfortable and warm. Secure too, that's the main thing. Can't be got by anyone, man or beast in here'.

Sheila Hines, a smartly dressed lady in her mid thirties, walked down The Strand carrying a red leather suitcase, her high stiletto heels making a decidedly clip clopping noise as she walked briskly along the pavement. She stopped briefly at a newspaper stand and bought a copy of 'The Evening Standard', opening her obviously expensive crocodile handbag to pay the news vendor.

Sheila tossed her beautifully coiffured auburn hair back in a rather vain fashion as she entered Charing Cross Mainline Station, at the same time scanning the departure boards for a sign of the next train to Rickmansworth. 'Platform 2' she read, 'leaving at 8.50p.m'.

She sighed deeply. 'Time for a coffee'. What a day she'd had. She'd met bag ladies before but the one she had encountered today had really saddened her. Despite her vanity Sheila was a kind, compassionate person 'Sometimes' she pondered, 'I'm almost ashamed that I've had it so good. A career, affluence, loving husband, friends and never a day in hospital'. She certainly felt guilty at how well off she was in comparison to her. She paused, she was thinking of the bag lady again 'Poor old soul. I hope there is something I can do to help such people. But not, God forbid, giving the wrong sort of charity. No, better to show them that they are accepted. Let them know they're ok, worthwhile as themselves in their own choice of life, identity'. Sheila finished her coffee. Approximately one and a quarter hours later, she was hailing a cab outside of Rickmansworth Station. 'The Cedars on Redman Street' she said to the cab driver. 'It's about halfway up on the left hand side, there is a street light right outside'.

She bundled inside the front door, throwing her velvet coat onto a vacant peg in the hallway and placing her red suitcase onto the nearby settee. Moving quickly, she hurriedly plugged in the kettle, measured a teaspoon of decaff coffee into a mug together with a small amount of semi-skimmed milk from the fridge. Carrying the coffee over to her desk in the lounge, she switched on her computer and began to type. Her eyes fell on to the red suitcase as the words appeared on the screen in bold print. The suitcase had sprung open. A battered looking felt hat and some greenish, wispy grey hair were staring back at her. Some fingerless gloves had fallen onto the settee. She laughed out loud as she turned back to the computer screen and read back what she had typed. 'Annie, a day in the life of a bag lady'.

Rough Justice

Rough   Justice

Nina hurriedly placed the violets in a
vase leaving deep footprints along the muddy
path which ran alongside the grave and
entered the little Chapel situated in the middle
of the cemetery.

Anxiously she glanced behind her as she
went to kneel at the altar rail. She felt the pain
of guilt tear into her soul, as if suddenly for the
first time, the awareness of what she had done
dawned on her.

Not that she had hated Stephen. In fact
she had really quite liked him but she believed
that he had deserved to die. Nina reasoned
with her sense of justice. In her mind he had
betrayed her daughter. That was unforgivable.
In Nina's mind, had she known about it,
Anna's life would have been ruined. Therefore
there was no way that Stephen should have
been allowed to live.

It had been so simple, maybe too simple,
perhaps walking along that cliff top path
with Stephen and Anna near their home that
evening. There had been few people about.
There never was along that particular stretch

of coastline.

Nina was certain that Anna was unaware of Stephens' affair but she herself knew. She had seen and watched them over a period of months, even going to the extreme of hiring an outside of town private detective. It had proved true. Nina was desperate that Anna would never know. Above all else, she was utterly determined that Anna would not suffer the kind of agony she herself had suffered. No, it was better this way and so, as they walked along the cliff that early May morning, she had allowed herself to drop behind Anna and Stephen so that Anna was in front as they came to the narrow unguarded stretch of path, she had pushed Stephen with all her might over the edge. He gave a quick, unbelieving stare as he fell and in a split second she had reached out automatically in a sort of reflex action to prevent his fall. But it was too late. He lost his balance and with a scream, toppled headlong to the awaiting rocks below. Nina knew instinctively that Anna had never suspected for an instant that it was anything other than an accident.

And now Nina paused at the altar rail in the Chapel with the realisation that this guilt and remorse was giving her such anguish. This was something she had not bargained for!

Her mind went back. She had met her own husband Paul, at school and had loved him ever since their first class together. She had always known that they made an odd looking pair, she, small, slim with raven black hair and huge brown eyes, he tall, muscular, with light sandy hair, mischievous eyes and a natural, permanent smile on his face, but she hadn't cared, she loved Paul and for her there was never anyone else.

They had married whilst still young. They had only one daughter Anna and when she left home to marry Stephen, Nina's love for Paul became even stronger.

One day Paul failed to return home from work. Nothing had seemed to be wrong but the next day when Paul still hadn't returned, she informed both the Police and 'Missing Persons'. Then the letter came. She couldn't even read the postmark and there was no address inside. It was the usual thing, a younger pretty secretary and that was that!

Nina found great difficulty in reading her own emotions. 'Did she feel bitterness or resentment? Jealousy perhaps'? Her hand gripped the altar handrail. All she remembered was the intense pain and loneliness, yes and sense of betrayal. But the suffocating loneliness and emptiness seemed to stretch from the top of her head right down to her toes.

And now she had discovered Stephen betraying Anna in a similar way. Nina realised that whatever demons were in her after Paul had left, had found their outlet in the killing of Stephen. She had become a murderess. My God, it was hard for her to take it in but the plain fact was that she had intentionally taken another life. It could have been Paul's but it was Stephen's. What difference did it make. The guilt she felt was no more endurable than the vacuum of emptiness.

Tears were blinding Nina's eyes as she stumbled out of the Chapel. 'Bob' she cried. 'I must go to Bob'. She felt safe with this man she had met two years ago when she had worked in a jewellery store and he had come in to examine some cuff-links that had been on display in the window.

'I'm divorced' he had told her simply when she had initially inquired into his earlier life.

Even then when she had looked into his eyes, she had instinctively known that this man was someone strong, dependable and trustworthy. A man she could and had already shared with. Her feelings had soon turned to love and although realising that Bob had not enabled her to forget the trauma of her past, she had learned to live with her demons until Stephens infidelity had somehow caused them to run riot in her disturbed mind.

It was raining again. Nina skirted along the pavement, oblivious to the rippling puddles which had accumulated where the concrete paving was uneven. She reached the taxi rank. Fortunately there was a taxi waiting which had just become vacant. She climbed in giving the driver directions and was soon running up the steps to Bob's second floor apartment.
Just as Nina was about to press the bell, Bob opened his front door.'

'Nina, I'm just going-----' Bob started to speak. 'Come in Nina' he said. She followed him into the lounge. He appeared to be agitated. 'Sit down Nina. I have been going to tell you for some time. I'm afraid I have been rather economical with the truth. I'm not divorced. My wife is well she's-----'.

Nina failed to hear Bob's last words. She rushed past him, arms and hands flailing, out of the door and down the steps.
She felt totally unreal as if she was watching

someone else playing out her life. This wasn't happening to her. It couldn't be!

The rain was now torrential but Nina seemed unaware of it. Her mind raced and zigzagged from one jagged thought to another like ill fitting pieces in a jigsaw puzzle. She ran in the direction of the railway station, fragments of sense intruding into her jumbled mind. At the time she had believed Stephen had deserved to die, so had Paul, but now she was in the wrong just as much as they had been.

Something in her was breaking. In her beleaguered mind, all rationality had disappeared. She knew what she must do, had to do. She reached the station and followed the railway track down. She saw the electric line. It was if it was beckoning to her, compelling her. 'Go on you can do it' a voice in her seemed to be saying.

She moved nearer the electric line, tears and perspiration mixed unrecognisably together on her cheeks. Her hands were trembling

'Hey What on earth are you doing'? In her confused state Nina was scarcely aware of the irate railway worker rushing towards her. 'Are you mad lady'? 'Oh my God what had you in mind'? He stared at her unbelievingly. Something suddenly seemed to shock Nina back to reality.

At that moment, another figure came into focus. 'Nina, Nina'. Bob came running towards them. Suddenly he stopped as if he was only just taking in the situation 'Nina' he spoke softly 'Its all right. She's ill. Pam, my wife she's very ill. She has had a cognitive brain disorder for five years. After a while I was unable to cope so I had her admitted to a long stay hospital. I'm so sorry Nina, I should have told you the truth but I was petrified I would lose you. I just see Pam on visits. Usually she doesn't recognise me but I have to go and see her now and then. You do understand don't you?. Please try and understand'. Bob was shaking nervously, rapidly, almost incoherently.

Nina exhausted and bewildered slumped into Bob's arms. Her mind still in turmoil but with pieces of the jigsaw just beginning to fit together. A feeling of safety slowly started to come over her. The rain had stopped. In the sky a small patch of blue was forming.

Bob gently kissed Nina on the head and mouthed a 'Thank you' to the astonished railwayman.

Bob slowly guided Nina carefully over the railway track and onto the adjoining road. He looked at Nina intently, perhaps knowingly. 'It's OK Nina, I'm here now. I'll always be here. I won't ever leave you Nina' he whispered.

A Chance Encounter

A Chance Encounter

Liverpool Street Station was busy it seemed, at the best of times. A hustling, bustling station with vast numbers of people herding in different directions, apparently oblivious of one another, their collective feet clip-clopping over a gigantic concrete sprawl. The big clock on the main station gave three loud 'Bongs'

'Almost like a call to prayer' John mused as he checked his watch.

'I can't believe I'm actually early for once' he thought to himself 'Time for a quick coffee'? He posed the question. 'Yes' he started in the direction of the Parisienne style café, at the end of platform 9. His broad frame casting an eerie shadow across the wide open space, his loud step seemingly out of tune with those of the people around him. He liked this particular café, round wooden tables covered with multi-coloured tablecloths. Rather 1950's he thought.

A loud speaker gave a slight cough followed by a mechanical sounding voice which was devoid of any emotion intoning 'The train standing at platform 6 to Wickford will be leaving in three minutes calling at

Ilford, Romford and Wickford only. Change at
Wickford for Battlesbridge, Woodham-Ferrers,
Fambridge, Althorne, Burnham-on-Crouch
and Southminster. John paid for his coffee
grimacing at how much profit the café must
now be making, found an empty table in the
corner of the room, opened up his copy of 'The
Guardian' and lit a cigarette. He inhaled deeply
and gave a sigh 'I wonder if these reports are
comprehensive enough'? He pondered. 'Why is
Clive so pedantic'? He frowned as he imagined
his boss scrutinising every detail 'longing' John
imagined, to find fault. He didn't like Clive.
Nothing ever pleased him. 'Still' he thought 'I
suppose I'm fortunate to have a job as well as
quite a tidy sum invested after----' His mind
went back to three years prior following the
break up of his marriage and the long period of
chronic depression that ensued and which had
culminated in the loss of his then job that had
not only been better paid but had been one
that he had actually enjoyed doing.

A wave of sadness came over him.
He suddenly felt old and grey. 'What had
happened is in the past, over. This is a new
chapter. I've turned a page' he muttered to
himself emphatically trying to convince himself
that this was so.

There was a sudden breath of air as he heard the café door pulled open. He looked up automatically.

'I can't believe it, Madeline, what on earth is she doing here'? He lifted himself out of his chair. 'Madeline' he called. 'Over here.'

Madeline glanced in the direction of the voice. She looked surprised, a hesitant smile formed on her face. 'Why John how are you'? she exclaimed. John momentarily took in the picture of his ex-wife standing in front of him. 'She looks tired' he thought 'Thinner, decidedly thinner and sad or is it fear? Come and join me. This really is quite extraordinary. What are you having? Coffee? I'll get it. You sit down' Madeline sat at John's table feeling rather awkward. 'I can't stay, Oh yes just a small cup please' She fidgeted with her handbag. John brought the coffee over and looked at Madeline. His eyes met hers. 'How are you'? he said. 'How long is it three years, nearly four'? Madeline looked embarrassed 'Four in August' she said 'I decided to have a day out at Romford Market' Madeline added, falteringly as if that explained everything.

She glanced at John, memories came flooding back almost as if her whole life with him was being played back on fast wind video.

'Have you seen the boys lately'? She took a sip of coffee 'Richard rings me up from time to time but I hardly ever see him and you know Malcolm never was very good at keeping in touch. I'm fortunate if I get a letter, maybe once in 9 months and I haven't got e-mail'. Her voice trailed off. 'No' said John 'My contact with them is even less'.

They fell silent 'Do you remember that midnight barbecue we all had, oh, it must be 7 years ago, eight? You know at Creeksea when we literally set fire to that row of bushes. Oh and that bull that cornered us on that walk. When was that? Walk? more of a chase I'd say'

'I remember more intimate things like climbing into the bath with you, especially that time when, in my haste, I threw the transistor radio in the bath and put the sponge on to the window sill to listen to'.

She laughed 'nervously' John thought. Suddenly Madeline became serious 'I threw him out' she said 'It's over, he drank and he---' her voice tailed off.

'Did he hit you? He did didn't he the swine?

Maddy, why did you leave me for him in the first place? Was I ever unkind to you? We weren't short of money. I was never unfaithful'.

Her eyes widened as she realised John had used his pet name for her.

'You were never there John. You became so engrossed in your work, we came to a point where you didn't appear to need me anymore. I grew bored, lonely. Simon represented freedom, an escape from the emptiness. I felt that my life was ebbing away, day after day, month after month I was in a kind of prison but I would never have had the courage to go off on my own. The boys had left home. I tried to explain it to you but you just never seemed to understand. I felt trapped, like a rabbit in a snare. I never really loved Simon but he was interesting, colourful and exciting and now----' Madeline broke off suddenly.

'Now what Maddy'? John asked. He paused slightly. 'It wasn't by chance your coming here today was it? How did you, how could you know'?

'I rang your old firm. They said they had sent a reference to the office you work in now. It wasn't difficult to find out your regular movements. I had to see you John. I know that you have someone else. It's just that I felt compelled to tell you, to tell you that----'

'To tell me what'? said John. He went on before Madeline had a chance to interrupt.

'I worked those extra hours for you Maddy. I wanted you to have the best. I'm sorry if I had my values all upside down. I hadn't realised my time with you was more important to you than material things. No I haven't got a girl friend. You must be referring to Elaine. My office colleagues met her once at a firms do. It never really got off the ground and-----'

'It doesn't matter now anyway' Madeline interrupted him. 'John, there is no easy way to say this. I just didn't want you to hear it from the boys. I'm terminally ill John, cancer. The prognosis is pretty bad. Maybe another year, two if I'm careful' Her mouth quivered involuntarily, tears smarted in her eyes. 'I'm so sorry John. You see despite everything I never stopped loving you. Oh don't worry. I'm not asking to come back but I'm frightened, so frightened'. Her hands were clenched, nails biting into them.

John looked at Maddy intently, his eyes mirroring the compassion he felt rising up inside him.

'Oh Maddy' was all he could utter. She looked at him imploringly. The tears were now streaming down her cheeks. 'Maddy' he repeated, touching her hand.
She got up suddenly and rushed to the door.

He followed her out catching her arm. She turned to him, their eyes meeting.
Something bigger than himself, something maybe even outside of himself engulfed him, overwhelmed him. Years fell away.

'Maddy' he repeated yet again, this time more softly 'Let's go home'.

The Man

The Man

Peter first noticed the man as he arrived at the small open air taverna situated on the beach at Sidari. He was wearing khaki and green combat trousers with a very colourful T-shirt and brown walking boots. He thought there was something vaguely familiar about him. 'He looks a bit conspicuous' Peter thought.

The man stared back at Peter. His eyes were bright and had what appeared to be a faint mixture of disapproval on his face. Peter looked away and spread his daily newspaper on the table in front of him. Lighting a cigarette he drew on it deeply and beckoned a nearby waitress to his table to order his usual Turkish coffee.

He had decided to come to Greece after seeing a cheap charter flight advertised on the internet. Fortunately he had managed to acquire a couple of weeks holiday after completing a few months work for his local NHS Trust.

Suddenly a thought struck him. 'When was he last in Corfu? Must be almost thirty years ago' he decided. 'Oh yes he'd noticed

some changes. Many more hotels and
obviously far more people and heavier traffic.
But the atmosphere was as he had always
remembered it The great music and dance, the
colourful tavernas, the magic of the casino, the
regular throb and heartbeat of the island both
night and day, a natural extension of each
other, just a pulsating continuance of time
with no real sense of purpose, pure hedonism'.

Peter finished his coffee and his cigarette
and looked up. The man had disappeared
and the seat he had been occupying was now
vacant. Peter walked onto the beach stopping
to laugh at some young children burying each
other in the soft golden sands. He suddenly
remembered his niece Tracy doing that to
him on the sands at Formby only she had
completely covered him, with just two straws
sticking into his mouth and up through the
sand. He laughed to himself. 'I suppose that
had been quite dangerous. Tracy's married
now with two young children of her own' He
sighed. 'How time has flown'
There were several others on the beach
including some men ogling a pretty girl in a
bikini. Suddenly a shadow was cast in front of
him. He looked round. It was the man. 'Well'
he thought. 'He's brave. Well maybe I'd risk it
but I am not sure that many people would'?

The man was wearing the briefest pair of swimming trunks, the excess of his stomach overlapping his belt, the upper carriage of his chest drooping down to meet the area of profusion, this time the man definitely glared at him, the expression on his face clearly defiant. 'Why not'? It seemed to say.

Peter strode quickly back to the road, hailed a passing taxi and alighted in Corfu Town just a few metres from the local hospital. He had decided to stock up on his toiletry needs prior to returning to his hotel. As he stepped out of the pharmacy he was almost deafened by the wailing sound of an ambulance crew. The ambulance skidded to a halt outside the A and E part of the hospital. The back door of the ambulance flew open and two ambulance men appeared pulling down a stretcher.

A grey looking face, almost covered with a blanket protruded from the top. It was the man. As the stretcher bearers moved quickly into the hospital, he overheard two women talking together in English. 'Went after her he did, that girl, almost drowned himself.'

Suddenly Peter went numb, memories of his own near death by drowning flooded through his mind. It was. 1968 He'd gone

on a European tour with his then girl
friend Maureen, her brother and his wife.
After a long and arduous drive down from
Milan, they had all stopped at a place called
Viarregio on the Ligurian sea. They felt hot
and sticky and tired. Arriving at Viarregio the
sea had appeared blue, warm and inviting.
Unfortunately they failed to notice the storm
warning flags at each end of the beach.

Maureen had got into difficulties first
and he had swum out to save her. However,
he was not a strong swimmer and although
he reached Maureen and managed to get hold
of her, she had slipped through his fingers
as a large wave hit them. He then not only
lost Maureen but he, himself, would most
certainly have drowned had it not been for
the efforts of a small rescue boat which had
put out to sea to save him. He was certain
he had counted going under eight times and
remembered calling out to God for help. A God
in whom, at that time he did not believe. What
he did remember clearly was the ambulance
arriving and the flashing lights of the local
Press photographer eager to make the evening
edition. Maureen somehow managed to grab
hold of a small rock jutting out of the sea and
was ultimately rescued from there.

Peter sighed as he walked slowly back to his hotel, eyes cast down and deep in thought. He felt uncomfortable, strangely ill at ease and yes, frightened, 'but of what exactly'? He shook his head unknowingly. The man had stirred up a past he had wanted to forget. He tried to put it out of his mind as he wandered into the bar and ordered a whisky and soda.

Several days later, feeling considerably better, he ventured down the road to the local supermarket in order to buy cigarettes and his favourite Retzina.

Making his way to the long display unit where the wines and spirits were all neatly stacked, he instinctively gave a glance at the person immediately to his right. It was the man. He found himself flushing with irritation and annoyance. 'Why was this man having such an adverse effect on him'? He was about to speak to him when his eyes noticed the contents of the man's shopping trolley. One small loaf of bread, a litre carton of milk, an onion, three or four carrots, and a tiny pack of potatoes. 'Obviously on his own' Peter thought. 'He looks lonely'. Suddenly a wave of guilt swept over him and sorrow for the man. Summoning up courage to say something to him, he turned but the man had disappeared.

He searched the check-outs along the various aisles up to the exit but the man was nowhere to be seen. 'I've a feeling this isn't the last I have seen of him' Peter muttered to himself. The following evening he went to see a film at the local classic cinema. 'Phaedra' Peter had seen it years ago and remembered how much he had enjoyed Melina Mercouri's performance.

He took his seat near the front and lit a cigarette. As the match flared he took a sharp intake of breath. There was the man in the row opposite only this time he had an attractive young looking girl with him.

Just as the adverts were coming to a close and 'Phaedra' was about to start there was a commotion, muffled voices but obviously agitated. Peter heard a girls shrill voice 'No I won't' and 'You can't and that's it'. He glanced to his side. The man and the girl appeared angry, the girl close to tears.

Suddenly her seat banged and she ran noisily up the aisle, the man looking sad and embarrassed lowered himself more deeply into his seat, his face gazing intently onto the cinema screen but registering despair. Peter recollected the awful final row Helen and himself had just two months short of their proposed wedding day. Pressures and commitments on both sides had become too intense, the arguments had become more frequent, when suddenly, without any obvious warning she'd said 'Perhaps it would be a relief if we split up'? He'd walked away without uttering a word. Many times he had tried to re-kindle the relationship but in spite of their mutual love for each other that day something had died. Oh they'd confessed polite forgiveness to each other and for a bit they remained in contact but their relationship could never be the same. The wedding arrangements were cancelled and gradually their friendship petered out altogether and they lost touch.

After the film Peter hung around the foyer for a while hoping to make contact at last, with the man. 'He must have left by another exit'. He said to himself as he wearily walked his way back to the hotel. On arriving at the hotel lobby he slowly climbed up the spiral staircase to his second floor apartment and climbed sleepily onto his bed.
'Gosh, I'm tired' he thought. 'I really am exhausted' He lay back on his duvet watching the heavy metal fan slowly spinning in the draught from the open window.

'Why had he come to Corfu'? His mind went
back to the holiday he'd had there with Helen
all those years ago and the fun they'd had
together. Dear Helen, what a complete mess
he'd made of their relationship, they really
had loved each other deeply. 'Why hadn't this
been enough to carry them up and over the
obstacles'? He'd had others such as Maureen
and life was ok. He had his dogs, his friends,
his hobbies, his garden and so much for which
he was grateful but what was missing? 'Am
I not facing up to getting older on his own,
am I into some kind of denial'? His thoughts
overlapped each other. 'Peace' he thought, 'I
lack peace, that near drowning accident, my
own life saved by a hairs breadth, perhaps
that's why I've grabbed life by the handles as it
were and tried to live as though there were no
more tomorrow. Has it made me any happier I
wonder'?

Peter shrugged his shoulders and
thought again about the man. The look
of loneliness he'd had on his face in the
supermarket and the rejected look he'd noticed
when his young companion had stormed out of
the cinema. Peter knew all about rejection.
Ironical that in a few chance meetings he had
had with the man that he had noticed so many

parallels with his own life. Suddenly he knew what he must do. 'I must see him, maybe we can help each other'?

Grabbing a clean bath towel from the chest of drawers, he rushed into the bathroom. Climbing into the shower unit, he was about to turn on the taps, when he caught a reflection of himself in the full length mirror opposite. Peter drew in a sharp intake of breath, small beads of perspiration trickled down his forehead, his hands shook, as the person staring back at him from the mirror was the man.

The Valentine

The Valentine

Edwina pushed the lank of wispy grey hair under her somewhat battered hat and stared at her complexion in the mirror, rosy, wind worn cheeks, cracked lips and bushy eyebrows stared back at her. But her eyes although watery, still showed character, strength and more than a hint of humour. She wrapped the woolly scarf around herself, picked up a rather worn duffle coat and equally worn gloves, put them on and proceeded down the stone steps into the street below.

The air was icy and very cold this early February morning. 'Just what I need to aid and abet my rheumatism' Edwina laughed to herself. Really she enjoyed this sort of climate. It made her feel alive and even expectant, but of what she wasn't quite sure.

She had lived in the block of tenement flats in East London quite alone for almost thirty years. A long bout of ill health and a weak heart had forced her to retire from a career in Nursing many years ago. Her pension had been small but now at aged seventy four, the additional Government pension had long enabled her to eke out a fairly frugal lifestyle, but all the same, Edwina had decided, one sufficient for her needs.

Despite her circumstances, Edwina loved life and considered each new day an adventure. Nevertheless she could be shy and sometimes quite lonely. All the same she was kind and patient and although never nosy or gossipy, she had a genuine altruistic attitude towards her fellow 'earth travellers' as she liked to call people.

Today was no exception. 'I'll call in at the Day Centre.' Edwina decided. They always did cheap but excellent lunches. She couldn't buy and cook anything less expensive for herself, but she wouldn't have a pudding. No it was 'Treat Day', a day when Edwina would give into her one weakness, some may have called it 'Comfort Eating' but Edwina had a real passion for chocolate and to her a bar of chocolate two or three times a week was neither excessive or greedy.

After a delicious first course and what proved to be a somewhat chatty, although not particularly intellectually stimulating lunch, Edwina stepped out towards her local newsagents to buy her 'Treat'.

She made her way across the park

and stopped for a moment to watch the kids' skate-boarding, a poignant smile crossing her lips. She was amazed at the obvious skill they displayed, jerking the end of the skateboard down and round fearlessly with the typical confidence of youth.

She turned and smiled again. This time at the ducks slip sliding across a very frozen pond banked by moulds of turf where snowdrops and crocuses were already in bloom. She was thinking of Tom, but then was there ever a day when she didn't think of Tom?

'How proud she was that he had loved her so and indeed she him, but how cruel life was and how quickly and suddenly her happiness had turned to sorrow, like a beautiful painting being slashed with a vicious knife'!

She broke off her thoughts as now she had reached the newsagents and was staring at a colourful display of valentine cards that had been carefully arranged for maximum effect in the shop window.

Memories came rushing back to her, 'I know you know it's from me' Tom had said 'And you are not supposed to know who has sent you a valentine but this one, this year, is special'.

Tom had regularly sent her a valentine card usually unsigned, just for fun, although Edwina had always known it was from him. However this one was bigger, glossier with huge red hearts entwined together beautiful red roses. She had instinctively got the message even before Tom had a chance to continue speaking. 'You do want to marry me, don't you Edwina'? he had said almost apologetically. Edwina paused in her thoughts. Fifty-Four years ago. She had been just twenty and the year 1939.

Tears, seemingly from nowhere smarted in Edwina's eyes as she entered the shop. The very same day they had got engaged and within a year, married. But within three years Tom was gone. 'Missing in action, presumed dead' the formal clinically worded telegram had said. There never was a proper funeral. Edwina purchased her chocolate bar and resolutely made her way back to her flat.

A wind chill factor had added a further element to the cold and Edwina tightened her scarf closely around her neck.

She climbed the few steps to her doorway, entered, lit the gas fire and boiled a kettle 'Where is that box'? she exclaimed.' Letters, cards, I know that valentine is in there somewhere'

Suddenly it seemed imperative to find it. She scrambled wildly, haphazardly through the box full of papers and cards. A tap on the door. 'Oh excuse me butting in' Ben said. 'Are you alright'? he added as he noticed Edwina's tear stained face and somewhat dishevelled appearance.

'Oh yes yes' she said vaguely. She looked up at Ben. 'You are my new neighbour aren't you'? We nodded to each other the other day. How are you settling in'? she added politely.

'Fine, Oh fine, I just thought it would be nice to make your acquaintance properly, but I can come back later if it is not convenient'?

'No, No I am just making tea. Please stay and have a cup. I am just looking for something' She forced a laugh, 'A valentine actually a special one, my husband, my late husband, gave to me. He died a very long time ago' she added lamely 'killed in the war'.

'I'm so sorry, perhaps if we turn the box right out' Ben said 'then you can----, Oh there it is' said Edwina. 'That's it, that's the one'. She picked up the card. 'I'm so sorry' Edwina said, weakly as now the tears had gained control and were beginning to stream down her face. 'No please don't go' said Edwina as Ben made a turn. 'I'll be alright. Please, have your tea, sugar'?

'You must be on your own next door' said Edwina. 'I know these are only single occupancy flats, My wife died of cancer three years ago' said Ben answering her question. 'I'm retired now, ex-school teacher, kind of made up for having no kids of our own. When Della died I thought I would give up teaching. I hadn't put much money by but well the classroom is not the same these days. I couldn't cope without Della's support'.

Edwina glanced at Ben. 'About sixty, no more' she thought. She took in his angular face and greying hair. 'He has strength' she thought 'Even if he doesn't realise it himself.' Ben's kindly eyes mirrored the compassion he extraordinarily had already begun to feel for this woman he had only just met.

They talked together over cups of tea and biscuits. The clock ticking over the mantelpiece seemingly in time with their quiet hesitant conversation. Ben glanced at his watch. 'Gracious, I've been here nearly an hour and a half' he said. 'I had better go. I am still unpacking you know. May I call again'?

'Please do' said Edwina. 'Just knock. I am usually in most days after 3p.m.'

Edwina carefully repacked her box of

letters and cards and read and re-read the valentine. 'See you again one day Tom' she said as she replaced the valentine back into the box. This time in a position where she knew she would find it more easily.

She lay back in her chair and dozed. It was dark and quiet. Suddenly there was a tap on the door. 'It's only me' Ben said. 'Look, please don't think I'm being impertinent. You see I am a book lover and 'Readers Digest' have just sent a book to me via 'White Arrow' I'd given them my new address you see' He paused. 'It's just that they have sent this with it. It's a purple orchid. Well chaps are not usually much ones for flowers so I thought you might like it. Please don't be offended' He looked at her enquiringly?

'Come in Ben' said Edwina smiling. 'It's two sugars isn't it'?